Wag!

Consultants

Ashley Bishop, Ph.D.

Sue Bishop, M.E.D.

Publishing Credits

Dona Herweck Rice, *Editor-in-Chief*
Robin Erickson, *Production Director*
Lee Aucoin, *Creative Director*
Tim J. Bradley, *Illustrator Manager*
Chad Thompson, *Illustrator*
Sharon Coan, *Project Manager*
Jamey Acosta, *Editor*
Rachelle Cracchiolo, M.A.Ed., *Publisher*

Teacher Created Materials
5301 Oceanus Drive
Huntington Beach, CA 92649-1030
http://www.tcmpub.com

ISBN 978-1-4333-2925-8

Printed in Malaysia. THU001.50393

bag

I like this bag.

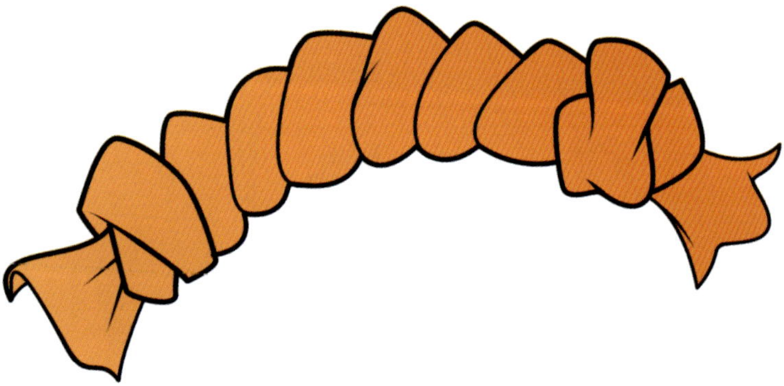

rag

I like this rag.

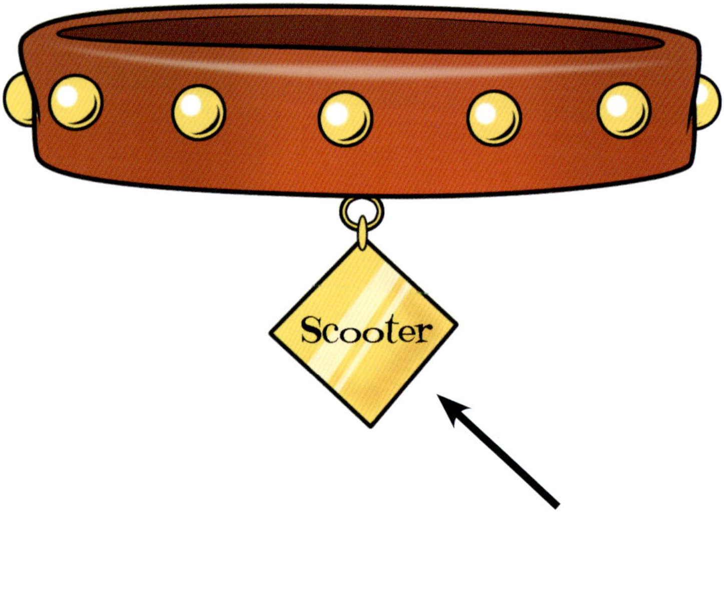

tag

I like this tag.

wag

I like this wag.

Wag! Wag! Wag!

Glossary

bag

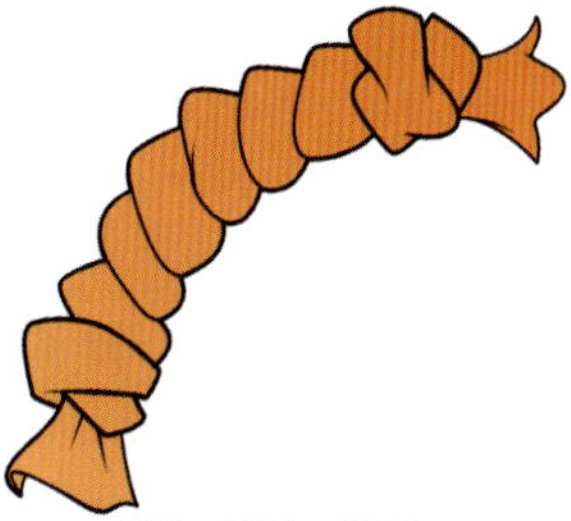

rag

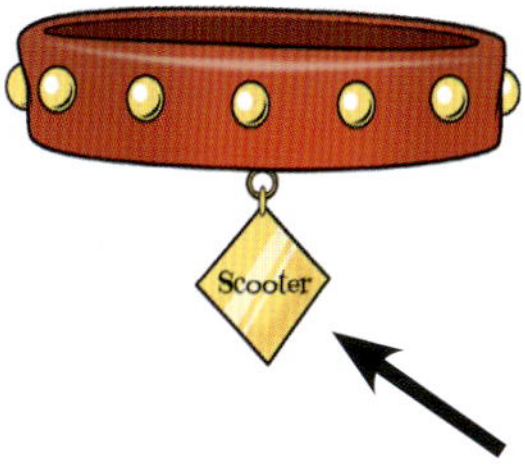

tag

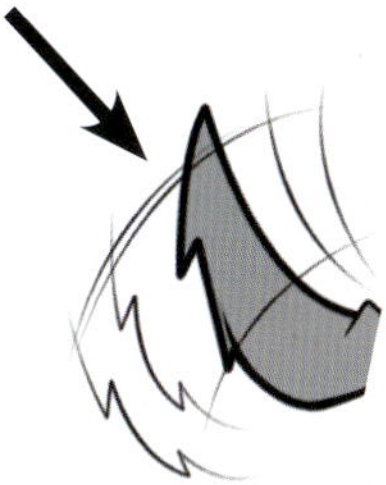

wag

Sight Words

I **like** **this**

Extension Activities

Read the story together with your child. Use the discussion questions before, during, and after your reading to deepen your child's understanding of the story and the rime (word family) that is introduced.

The activities provide fun ideas for continuing the conversation about the story and the vocabulary that is introduced. They will help your child make personal connections to the story and use the vocabulary to describe prior experiences.

Discussion Questions

- What is in the bag in the story? What items do we have at home that are in a bag?
- What does the dog do with the rag in the story? What can we use a rag for?
- Who wears the tag in the story? Why do dogs wear tags?
- What wags in the story? When does a dog wag its tail?

Activities at Home

- Have your child pick items at home that are interesting, and use the "I like this ________." phrase appropriately while talking about them.
- Talk about the different bags that people use at home. Have your child look for different kinds of bags.